Contents

Don't Look Now

DAPHNE DU MAURIER

Level 2

Retold by Derek Strange
Series Editors: Andy Hopkins and Jocelyn Potter

Pearson Education Limited
Edinburgh Gate, Harlow,
Essex CM20 2JE, England
and Associated Companies throughout the world.

ISBN 0 582 41771 6

Typeset by RefineCatch Limited, Bungay, Suffolk
Set in 11/14pt Monotype Bembo
Printed in Spain by Mateu Cromo, S.A. Pinto (Madrid)

Published by Pearson Education Limited in association with
Penguin Books Ltd., both companies being subsidiaries of Pearson Plc

For a complete list of the titles available in the Penguin Readers series please write to your local
Pearson Education office or to: Marketing Department, Penguin Longman Publishing,
5 Bentinck Street, London W1M 5RN.

Introduction

He looked up and found the second woman, with the whiter hair, looking at him with strangely empty eyes again, waiting for her tall friend to come back. He did not like it. Why did she look at him like that? It worried him.

John and Laura are on holiday in Venice. Their daughter, Christine, is dead and they want time to forget, time to live again and be happy.

But it is not going to be easy. When they see the two tall, thin old women, they know that something is wrong. And then the women say Christine is here, with them, and there is something she wants to say . . .

Daphne du Maurier was born in 1907 in London. She did not go to school but had lessons at home. Her family were quite rich but she always wanted to live by writing. She did this after she wrote *Rebecca* (1938), her most famous book. She married in 1932 but she was never happy with her husband. For most of the time she lived in Cornwall, in the south-west of England. Many of her best stories are about this place. When she was older, she lived in her house at Fowey, by the sea. She loved walking, gardening and watching birds. She died in 1989, when she was eighty-one.

After *Rebecca* she wrote fourteen more books and she also wrote many stories. *Don't Look Now* is a story from a book called *Not After Midnight* (1971). *The Birds* is another famous story. It is a Penguin Reader too.

There are many films of her books and stories. Alfred Hitchcock's films of *Rebecca* (1940) and *The Birds* (1963) are famous. *Don't Look Now* is also a film (1973).

'Don't look now. Behind you,' John said to his wife. 'Don't turn round quickly. They'll know you're looking at them.'

Don't Look Now

'Don't look now,' John said to his wife, 'but there are two old girls two tables away, looking at me all the time. I don't like it. There's something very strange about their eyes.'

Laura, immediately interested, slowly turned her head.

'Behind you,' John said. 'Don't turn round quickly. They'll know you're looking at them.'

Laura turned round more, caught the eye of the man to bring them some more coffee now, and then looked quickly at the table behind her before she turned back again. She was red in the face, excited, wanting to laugh.

'They're not old girls, John,' she said. 'They're men, dressed up in women's clothes. Very strange, I must say!'

She must not laugh, John thought. He quickly took her glass and gave her some more wine.

'I don't think they saw you looking,' he said, giving her the glass. 'Here, drink some water. You mustn't laugh. Perhaps they're dangerous. Murderers or something, going round Europe, changing their clothes in each place. You know, sisters here on Torcello this morning; brothers tomorrow, or tonight, back in Venice. Running from the police, perhaps.'

'Murderers?' asked Laura.

'Yes. Murderers. But why me? Why are they looking at me all the time? Oh no! The sister with the white hair has got her eye on me again.'

The man brought the coffee and took away the fruit, so Laura had time to drink some of her wine, to stop herself wanting to laugh so much.

'I don't think they're murderers. I think they're two old

1

women from Australia or somewhere, in Venice on holiday together. Called Tilly and Tiny, or something.'

Suddenly, for the first time on this holiday, she was like the old Laura again, trying not to laugh and going red in the face, making up stories about people sitting near them in restaurants, visiting old churches and looking at famous pictures in different cities with him again. Suddenly she didn't look sad and afraid any more. Perhaps, he thought, perhaps she's starting to get better, starting to laugh and live again. Perhaps she will begin to forget and then we can go on together, he thought.

'You know,' said Laura, 'that was a very good lunch.'

Good, he thought, that's better . . . and very quietly he said to her, 'One of them is standing up, looking at the back of the restaurant. Do you think she's going to change her clothes or hair again?'

'Don't say anything,' she answered. 'I'll follow her and see. Perhaps she's got a bag out there, with all their different clothes in it. Where is she now?'

'Coming past our table in a minute,' he told her.

The woman was not very unusual, when you saw her from near to. Tall, with a long thin nose and short hair. About sixty-four or -five, he thought, with a man's shirt and a heavy, long brown skirt. Strong black shoes, good for walking. But the interesting thing was that there were two of them – two, the same, like sisters. Her friend's hair was whiter, that was all. Trying not to laugh again, Laura stood up, ready to follow.

'I mustn't laugh,' she said. 'Don't look at me when I come back or I know I'll laugh.' She took her handbag and walked away from the table, following the tall woman to the door at the back of the restaurant.

John had some more coffee, lit a cigarette and watched the other people sitting in the sun outside the little hotel, finishing their lunch. 'So perhaps the holiday *is* helping Laura to forget, to

*'One of them is standing up, looking at the back of the restaurant.
Do you think she's going to change her clothes or her hair again?'*

be happy again, to go on living without Christine,' he thought.

'She'll get better very slowly,' the doctor said. 'They always do, but it takes time. Give her time. You still have your young son to think about, and you're still young, you and Laura. You'll have other children, another daughter, perhaps.'

So easy to say that . . . she loved Johnnie, their son, but Christine . . . Christine was everything, the world, to Laura. And he knew Laura too well: another child, another daughter, yes, but not Christine; not the same. Not the beautiful little girl with dancing eyes and thick black hair, now dead.

He looked up and found the second woman, with the whiter hair, looking at him with strangely empty eyes again, waiting for her tall friend to come back. He did not like it. Why did she look at him like that? It worried him. He took a cigarette and played with it in his fingers. He knew her eyes were on him all the time. He looked at his watch. Laura's taking a long time, he thought. More than ten minutes now. Where is she? What's she doing in there? Suddenly, the tall woman walked slowly past their table, stood next to her friend and said something to her quietly. John could not hear the words. Her friend stood up and they moved away together, arm in arm through the tables, out across the garden of the hotel. Laura came out of the door at the back and stood there watching them leave, her face very white.

'Well, you took your time . . .' he began, and stopped, seeing her face. Something was wrong. She walked carefully to their table and sat down. He quickly pulled up a chair next to her.

'What happened? What did she do?' he asked. 'What is it, Laura? Tell me. Are you ill?'

She turned and looked at him, slowly looking happier.

'She isn't dead, John. She's here with us. That's why they looked at us all the time, those two sisters. They could see Christine.'

Oh no, he thought. It's what I was afraid of. She's going out of her head. What do I do? How can I help her?

'I must tell you, love,' Laura went on. 'I'm so excited, so happy! When I went out there, I was washing my hands and suddenly the tall woman turned to me and said, "Don't be unhappy. My sister saw your little girl. She was there with you at the table, between you and your husband, laughing." She said Christine wanted us to know she was here with us. John? You don't believe me, do you? But that's what she said. I'm so happy. I can't tell you how happy I am. I know she was right, that woman. Her sister can see things other people cannot see . . . she said Christine was in that blue-and-white dress she wore for her birthday last year. Remember?'

What could he say? How could he answer her? She sat there,

'What happened. What did she do?' he asked. 'What is it, Laura?
Tell me. Are you ill?'

not crying, not excited. Quiet. Smiling at him, looking happy for the first time in days.

'Yes, Laura. I . . .' What could he say?

She stood up. 'Come on. We must see the church here on Torcello, now that we're here.'

So they left the restaurant, and walked slowly through the market with its clothes and fruit and cheap sunglasses, across the square and into the church. Inside, it was dark, colder than in the sun in the square. They moved slowly along with the other people, Americans and Germans and Japanese, all talking to each other quietly. Then suddenly John saw them again, the two sisters, standing together in a dark corner, away from all the other people, looking at him again. He wanted to get out, get away from the two strange women, back to Venice as quickly as they could. He took Laura's arm and began to push her in front of him, through all the people, to the door. She did not want to leave so soon, but she thought he was not interested in seeing the church, so she said nothing. They came out into the sun, walked down to the water, and found their boat, waiting to take them back to Venice again. They took their places in the boat and he put one arm round her. She smiled up at him. 'What a good day! I'll never forget it. Never. You know, love, I think I'm starting to have a very, very good holiday.' And she laughed.

He smiled back at her, happily. It's going to be all right, he thought. She's coming back to me again. Everything will be the same as before between us. Venice will bring us together again, help us to start living again without Christine. We'll go out and find somewhere different for dinner this evening, he thought, not the place we usually go to. Somewhere new.

Their hotel was a small, comfortable place, near the Grand Canal. The man at the front desk smiled and gave them their key. From the window of their room they could see the boats coming and going along the canal in the late afternoon. John turned on

*Suddenly John saw them again, the two sisters, standing together
in a dark corner, away from all the other people.*

the hot water in the bathroom, wanting a bath before the evening. Now, he thought as he went back into the bedroom, is the time to make love, to be together again after all these weeks. She understood, opened her arms to him and smiled.

'The thing is, love,' she said later, doing her hair in front of the looking-glass, 'I'm not very hungry. Shall we have a quiet evening and eat here in the hotel?'

'No, no. Let's go out. Let's go and find a small, dark place where the Italians eat when they're in love. We can sit hand in hand, drinking wine together, waiting for midnight.'

They went out laughing into the warm quiet night. 'Let's walk,' he said, 'so that you're hungry by the time we find somewhere good to eat.'

So they walked, and soon they lost themselves in the small dark backstreets of the city, away from the sounds of the boats and the water. The houses stood tall and dark above them, their windows closed. John did not know where they were. Laura thought they were somewhere near the church of San Zaccaria, and thought there was a restaurant in a small street next to the church. They were at the corner of another dark, empty street, the same as all the others, when they heard the cry – a dying cry, suddenly stopped. It came from one of the houses with its windows closed, black and dead. But which one? They stopped and listened.

'What was that?' said Laura, worried and afraid.

'Someone with too much wine inside them, perhaps,' said John quickly. 'Come on.' But it wasn't like that, he knew.

They walked away quickly up the street, Laura in front, John behind. Suddenly something caught his eye: someone moving from the dark door of one of the houses, climbing into a small boat in the water next to the house. A child, a little girl, of only five or six, wearing a short coat. John stopped and watched her. She jumped from the first boat to another and to another, across

A child, a little girl of only five or six, wearing a short coat. John stopped and watched her. It took only a minute.

the water, and then to the door of an old black-looking house, through its black door, and away. It took only a minute.

Laura didn't see, he thought. He was happy about that. He heard her feet coming back down the street.

'What are you doing? I nearly lost you.'

'Sorry,' he said. 'I'm coming.'

He took her arm and they walked fast along the little street and came out into a small square behind a church. Not a church he knew. They walked on across the square, into another street, down it, more and more lost. Suddenly, in front of them they saw lights and people walking in front of another beautiful church. San Zaccaria. He turned and smiled at her.

'Let's go and find your restaurant, then. That was quite exciting, wasn't it?' he said.

They saw the word 'Ristorante' in orange lights at the corner of a street across the square, and soon they were inside, with the people eating and drinking, men in white shirts and black trousers pushing past chairs, carrying plates of food, opening bottles of wine, shouting back to the kitchen in fast Italian that they could not understand. They sat at a table in the corner and John looked about him while Laura looked at the menu.

Then he saw them, the two old sisters, taking their places at a table across the room. He was immediately uncomfortable. He wanted to leave, to get out of the place, but Laura was happily looking at the menu, waiting for her drink to arrive. Why were the two old women in the same restaurant? Of all the hundreds of different restaurants in Venice, why were they here, in *this* restaurant? And why did Laura want to come to a restaurant near the church of San Zaccaria? Did she know the two sisters ate here, and wanted to meet them again?

Laura looked up from the menu and started to look round the room. She saw them and gave a little cry.

'Oh John! Look! It's those two strange sisters we met on Torcello this afternoon, sitting at that table over there. They're looking over here. I must go and talk to them for a minute. I must tell them how happy they made me today.'

Before he could stop her, she got up and, moving quickly past the man arriving with their drinks, walked across the room. He watched her stop by their table, smiling, then pull up a chair and sit down with them. All right, John thought. I'll have a good evening without you, then. And he ordered another drink and a bottle of cold white wine to have with his food. He watched the three women at the table across the room. Laura, listening to the taller sister talking, sometimes asking a question. The smaller sister with white hair said nothing, but looked quietly across at his table.

What do they want to talk to Laura for? he thought, beginning his second drink. I'm not happy about it. Why are they after my wife like this, following her, telling her things about Christine?

His food came and he started to eat, but then he pushed the plate away, suddenly not hungry any more. Then Laura was back, sitting down again at their table, starting to eat her own food, some fish, not saying anything, not seeing that he was not eating. She finished her fish, drank a little of her wine and began to speak.

'I know you won't believe it, love,' she said, 'but the sister with the white hair said she saw Christine with us again, after we left the restaurant on Torcello this afternoon, in the church there. She said she thought Christine wanted to tell her something about us, that we were in danger here in Venice. Christine is worried about us. She wants us to leave here as soon as we can . . . John? Why don't you say something?'

'Because you're right. I don't believe it. I don't believe anything your two old sisters tell you.' He was angry now.

11

These two old girls could not start telling him where to go and what to do on his holiday.

'Please believe them, John. I do. They said that Christine wanted us to leave Venice immediately, tomorrow. Then we'll be all right, they said.'

John just laughed and took another glass of wine for himself.

'There's not much more for us to see here, John. I'd like to see some of the other famous Italian cities. And I do believe that Christine is trying to tell us to go.'

'Right. OK. That's it. We'll go. We'll go back to the hotel now and tell them that we're leaving in the morning. Do you want anything more to eat now?'

'Oh, John,' said Laura unhappily, 'don't be angry. Don't take it like that. Look, why don't you come over and meet them? They could tell you about it themselves and perhaps you'd believe it all then. It's you they're talking about, you know. Christine is more worried about you than about me. That's what they said. And the strange thing is that the shorter sister, with the white hair, says that you can see things other people can't see, too. She says you don't know it, but you can. She says you sometimes see Christine yourself, but you don't know you're doing it.'

'One thing I *can* see, Laura, is that I want to get out of this restaurant now, immediately. Then perhaps we can talk about leaving Venice, when we're back at the hotel.'

Laura was unhappy, saying nothing, playing with her handbag as they waited to pay and leave. John looked quickly across at the sisters' table two or three times as they waited, and saw them eating big plates of food, with a bottle of good red wine. Not very strange, he thought. Just two hungry women. I don't believe a word they say. He paid and pushed back his chair.

'Are you ready?' he asked.

Laura was unhappy, saying nothing, playing with her handbag as they waited to pay and leave.

'I'm going to say goodbye to them,' said Laura, her unhappy mouth and eyes looking for a minute like their little dead child's. She was always very like Christine when she was angry, he thought sadly.

She went through the tables and chairs, across to the two sisters, and he left the restaurant before her, to wait for her outside.

Outside, waiting for Laura to come out, it started to rain. People walked past quickly, their heads down. The streets were nearly empty; there were not many people in the square by the church now – it was quite different from the warm, comfortable evening before they got lost and went into the little restaurant, happy and hungry. This is what the people who live here see, he thought, when there are no British and Americans and Germans in the city, in winter, when everything is quiet.

Laura came out and they started to walk back to their hotel. In the Piazza San Marco it started to rain more heavily and they stopped in the door of some shops, out of the rain. Nobody was at the café tables in the square now. Everything was wet. They're right, he thought, when they say Venice is dying. Soon it will all be under water, an under-sea city, and people will come to visit it in boats, looking down at the buildings and churches below them, under the water, like a lost world. He was sad. The evening started so happily, laughing together, but it is ending like this, in the rain, with not a word between us.

When they arrived back at the hotel, John asked for their key and the man gave him an envelope at the same time. He opened it immediately. It was from the head of their son's school, in England. He read

Johnnie in city hospital here. Taken ill yesterday. Do not worry, but doctor told me to let you know.

Yours

    Charles Hill.

He read it again, then walked slowly over to the door where Laura stood, waiting for him. He gave her the letter.

'This came when we were out,' he said. 'Not very good, I'm afraid.'

She read it and looked up.

'Well, that's it, then, isn't it? We can't stay, can we? We must leave Venice and go back to be with Johnnie. It's Johnnie who's in danger, not us. This is what Christine wanted to tell the two old sisters.'

◆

14

When they arrived back at the hotel, the man gave him an envelope.
He opened it immediately and read.

First thing the next morning, John tried to telephone Mr Hill, the head of their son's school in England. His wife answered and said that her husband was at the hospital, visiting Johnnie, but he could call back in an hour. John gave her the hotel's number. Then he told the hotel that they wanted to leave later in the morning, and they started to put some of their things into their bags, ready to go. They did not talk about the two old sisters, or about the day before. Laura believed that the letter from England, about Johnnie being in hospital, was what Christine wanted to tell them. But she said nothing; she knew John did not believe it. They had breakfast and talked about how they could get home, how they could get themselves and their car on the through train from Milan to Calais, and about how Mr Hill's letter said 'Don't worry'. The call from the school in England came when John was in the bathroom. Laura answered it. When John came in a minute or two later, she was still speaking, but he could see that she was worried.

'The doctor says Johnnie didn't have a good night last night,' Mr Hill said.

'He's worse than he was yesterday. That's nothing very unusual, the doctor says. But he's going to have a small operation today or tomorrow. We're very sorry about this, but perhaps . . . my wife and I thought perhaps you could come back, to be with him?'

'Oh yes, yes, as soon as we can. You're quite right,' Laura said.

'But please don't worry too much. The hospital here is very good, and the doctor knows what he's doing.'

'Yes,' said Laura, 'good . . .' and then stopped because John was behind her, trying to tell her something.

'We can try to get you on a plane, today, and then I can come back on the train with the car,' he said. 'Then you'll be there by this evening.'

'Yes,' she answered. And then to the telephone, 'We're going

When John came in a minute or two later, she was still speaking, but he could see that she was worried.

to try to get back as soon as we can, Mr Hill. I'm sure Johnnie will be all right in the hospital. Please thank your wife for helping him, too. Goodbye.'

She put down the telephone and looked round at all the books and coats and other clothes all over the room, waiting to go into their bags. The telephone went again. Laura, sitting next to it, picked it up again. It was the man from the hotel desk. He had places on the train to London for them and their car, for the next night.

'Look,' said Laura. 'I'm sorry, but can you get a place on today's plane from Venice to London, for me? One place. My husband will follow on the train with the car tomorrow, but one of us must be back in England by tonight.'

17

Her face was white with worry. She put the telephone down again.

'We lost Christine, but we're not going to lose another child,' she said.

'All right, love. It'll be all right . . .' He put his hand on her arm, but she pushed it away, so he turned back to his clothes and his bag. It was no good saying anything more. Better to let her go quickly on the plane, and for him to follow with the car. But then he had another thought.

'Perhaps we can fly back together,' he began, 'and I can come back later to get the car and drive it back through France . . .'

But she did not want that. It was too expensive. 'And we can't go off and leave all our things and the car here,' she went on. 'How will we get to and from the hospital, to visit Johnnie, without the car?'

She was right. It was only − well, he was as worried about Johnnie as she was, but he didn't want to say so.

She went down to the hotel desk to ask the man about the plane ticket; John finished putting his things into a bag. She telephoned up to the room from the desk a minute or two later.

'It's all going to be all right,' she said. 'There's a plane leaving from Venice to London in under an hour, and a boat is going from the Piazza San Marco for the airport in about ten minutes. I'll be in England by this afternoon.'

'I'll bring your bag down immediately, then,' he told her.

She was at the desk when he went down, looking happier, not so white and worried. She was leaving. He wanted to be leaving with her; he did not want to stay in Venice or drive to Milan without her, and the thought of the long hours on the train back to Calais from Milan the next night did not make him any happier. And he was worried about Johnnie, too.

They walked along to the Piazza San Marco, clean and

18

They walked along to the Piazza San Marco, clean and new-looking after the rain, and found the boat for the airport.

new–looking after the rain, and found the boat for the airport. People walked slowly past, warm, happy, looking up at the front of the beautiful big church, and boats came and went in the sun.

'I'll telephone you tonight from Milan,' he told her. 'Mr and Mrs Hill will give you a bed at the school, I think, so I'll phone you there later this evening, when you're back from the hospital.'

Laura put her arms round him for a minute and they stood together quietly before she climbed down into the boat with all the other English people going back to England after their holiday in Venice. She found a place next to a smiling man and his smiling wife, near the front of the boat. They started to talk to her immediately and she looked up at John, standing there watching her from the square.

The boatman called out something in Italian, and the boat began to move away across the water. He stood watching it, sad and lost inside himself without her, and soon her red coat was like the only small flower in a garden of darker colours, the greens and browns, of the clothes of the other people in the boat. He turned and walked away, back to the hotel, not seeing the sun on the city all round him.

There was nothing, he thought, looking at their bags, at Laura's second coat lying on the bed, nothing as sad as a hotel room with its last visitors leaving, before the next visitors arrive. He could see Laura here in so many things in the room. Her pen, now finished with, left by the telephone; her coffee cup on the small table by the window; a long hair on the bed, light now with the sun on it. He could hear the sound of the people and the boats outside, but she wasn't there to listen to or watch it all with him. It was all empty; the holiday was suddenly finished.

He left their bags ready and went down to the hotel desk, to pay. New people were there, talking to the man at the desk, sitting outside watching the boats on the Grand Canal, thinking about what to do that day.

John asked for an early lunch, here at the hotel, a place he knew, before getting the bags down to the boat at the Piazza and then across to the garage where their car was. He was hungry. But even in the hotel restaurant, things were different. There were new people at the table he and Laura usually had by the window, so he sat at a small table for one, away from the window, and could not see the canal or the people outside.

She's in the plane now, he thought, with all those other English people in their green and brown clothes, smiling and talking to her. He imagined Laura telling them about Johnnie in hospital, about him bringing the car back on the train. Well, those two strange sisters must be happy about it, he thought. We're leaving. Going home. That's what they wanted.

Lunch finished, he didn't sit with a cup of coffee and a slow cigarette at a table outside in the sun. He wanted to leave as soon as he could, to get the car and start for Milan. He asked someone to bring their bags down from the room, said goodbye to the people at the hotel desk, and, with the hotel boy carrying the bags behind him, he walked back to San Marco, to the boats. He found the right boat, got all the bags into it, paid the boy, and sat among the people, waiting to go. For a minute, sitting there before they started, he was sad to be leaving Venice. Will we come here again? he asked himself. Will we come back to finish this holiday, to be happier here some time later?

The boat moved out. He could see the famous square, with all its tall, white buildings in the sun, people on holiday, some wearing dark glasses, walking slowly together, stopping, looking,

21

talking. So much here that he knew now, to try and remember. Smaller and smaller. The boat moved away quite fast, up the Grand Canal, past the little red house where d'Annunzio lived, with its garden – 'our house' Laura called it – and turned left to the Piazzale Roma, so that they didn't go past some of the best places on the canal, like the Rialto.

Another boat went past them, and for a minute he wanted to jump into it, to go back to Venice again, to all that was now behind him. Then he saw her. Laura, there in the other boat in her red coat, and with the two strange sisters next to her, talking to her; Laura looking sad and lost. He didn't move; he was amazed. The other boat was past them now, so they couldn't see or hear him.

What happened? he asked himself. Why didn't she get the plane? And why didn't she phone me at the hotel before I left? She knew I was there. And now, why was she with those women again, looking worried and afraid? He could think of no good answers to all the questions in his head. Perhaps she wants to drive to Milan with me, after all, and is going back to the hotel to find me, he thought. The only thing to do was to telephone the hotel as soon as they arrived at the Piazzale Roma and tell her to wait there. Then he could go back and get her, get her away from those two old women.

When the boat arrived at the Piazzale Roma, everyone pushed to get off the boat, as usual. He found a man to take the bags and to look after them for five minutes when he went to telephone the hotel. He found the number and the right money and luckily the man he knew answered the telephone.

'. . . A mistake, I think,' he said. '. . . I don't understand . . . I think my wife is back at the hotel . . . She was with two friends ten minutes ago, coming back into Venice . . .' Could the man find her and ask her to wait there. 'I'll get a boat back into

Then he saw her. Laura, there in the other boat in her red coat,
and with the two strange sisters next to her.

*'I'll be as quick as I can.' The man with their bags stood waiting
for him to finish on the 'phone.*

Venice,' he said. 'I'll be as quick as I can.' The man understood
everything, and John put down the telephone.

The man with their bags stood waiting for him to finish
on the 'phone. The easiest thing now was to take all the bags
to the car in the garage, put them all in it and then
come back and get the next boat back to the hotel. The
minutes went by slowly, as he waited by the water for
the next boat to come, and all the time worrying, Why
didn't she get the plane? What's wrong? Why didn't she
telephone me? It was no good trying to imagine. She could
tell him everything when he got back to the hotel and found
her.

In San Marco, when they arrived half an hour later, there were more people than before. He walked quickly back to the hotel, in through the doors, ready to smile at Laura, waiting inside with her story to tell him. She was not there. He went to the desk. Luckily again, the same man was there.

'Is my wife here?' John asked.

'No, sir. I'm sorry, sir. She is not here.'

'That's very strange. I don't understand why not. She was on one of the boats coming back from the airport.'

'I don't know what to say, sir,' the man said. 'She was with friends, I think you said? Perhaps she is with them, at their hotel, and will come here later.'

'Yes. Well, two women we met on Torcello yesterday. We didn't know them before. We saw them again later, yesterday evening, at a restaurant here in Venice. I was amazed to see her with them today on the boat, and not at the airport or on her plane, where I thought she was.'

So where was she? It was after three now.

'Do you know where they are staying, sir?' the man asked, trying to help.

'No, I don't. And I don't know the names of these two women, but I think they were sisters. They looked nearly the same. But why go to their hotel, and not here? That's what I can't understand.'

'I'll tell you what I'll do, sir,' the man said. 'I'll telephone the airport and ask about that plane. Then we will know about that.'

'Yes, please,' said John. It was the only thing to do.

He lit a cigarette and walked up and down, waiting for the man to finish talking on the phone. It took a long time and the man's Italian was too fast for John to understand what he said. He finished and put down the telephone.

'Very strange, sir. The plane left on time, and everyone was on it,
they say. They think your wife was on it with the others.'

'Very strange, sir. The plane left on time, and everyone was on it, they say. They think your wife was on it with the others.'

John was quiet, more worried now than before. Where was Laura? Was she all right? The man looked worried too.

'Perhaps, sir, you made a mistake? Perhaps it was not your wife on the other boat, coming back from the airport?'

'Oh no,' said John. 'It was my wife. I know it was. She was wearing the same red coat she had on when she left here this morning.' He lit another cigarette and went out to look at the street, the canal, to look for a woman in a red coat . . . Laura was out there somewhere. At half-past four, he went back to the hotel desk.

'I can't wait here any more,' he said. 'I must try to get to Milan this evening. Please tell my wife, when she comes in, that I came back and waited.'

The man looked very worried now. 'Yes, sir. I will do that.'

John went out and began to walk back to the Piazza San Marco. He looked into all the shops and at all the café tables, looking for Laura's red coat or those two sisters, but he saw nobody he knew. The only thing to do was to try to find those sisters now. Their hotel could be anywhere, but perhaps they were at a small hotel somewhere near San Zaccaria, near the little restaurant they were at last night. So he walked slowly back to the little restaurant near San Zaccaria, and asked one of the men getting the tables ready for the evening about the two old sisters. The man said he remembered them, yes, but he was very sorry, he did not know where their hotel was.

John walked out into the street again. He was afraid now. How could he find Laura? And what did those two women want with her?

Suddenly he saw a police station and thought, this is it. I can't

27

'It's on the radio; everyone's talking about it. Woman found dead
somewhere near here last night. Killed with a knife.'

find Laura. I'm going inside to ask them to help me. He went inside.

There was another Englishman and his wife in there, waiting to speak to someone about a lost handbag. How could he tell them he wanted to speak to someone about a lost wife?

'They won't do much for us tonight,' the man said unhappily, 'not with this murderer somewhere out there.'

'Murderer? What murderer?' asked John.

'You don't know?' the man asked. 'It's on the radio; everyone's talking about it. Woman found dead somewhere near here last night. Killed with a knife. She was here on holiday, too, they say. It's not good for Venice, that isn't.'

A door opened and someone called the man and his wife away to talk about their lost handbag. John sat, remembering calling the two sisters 'murderers' at the restaurant on Torcello and laughing about it with Laura. Now Laura was not there and he could not find her; another woman was dead, murdered with a knife. He could not tell the police that he believed those two old sisters had his wife somewhere, wanted to kill her too, perhaps. What do I say, then? he thought. He looked at his watch. Half-past six.

Another door opened and a policeman asked him to go into a small office. He gave his name, the name of the hotel, etc, etc. Then he told the man about Laura, the two sisters, the plane to England and seeing her with them later, on the boat coming back into Venice. The man looked worried. John could see that he believed him.

'Please go back to your hotel now, sir,' the policeman said. 'We will telephone you there as soon as we know any more.'

He went back to the hotel and they gave him a room for the night, a small room at the back of the hotel. He washed and asked them to send half a bottle of nice cold wine up to his room. Then he tried to telephone England, to speak to Mr Hill again, to find out how Johnnie was. After a minute or two he heard Mrs Hill answer, saying, 'Hello?' He told her who he was.

'Oh, I'm so happy you rang. All is well here. Johnnie had an operation this morning, and the doctor says he'll soon be much better. So you mustn't worry any more. You can sleep well tonight. Now your wife's here with me, and she wants to speak to you. Bye.'

John sat up on the bed, amazed. He heard Laura say, 'John, John? Are you there?'

He could not answer. He could not believe it.

'Yes, I'm here,' he said quietly, after nearly a minute.

'Everything is all right here now,' she went on. 'Johnnie is sitting up in bed again after his operation and he's quite comfortable in the hospital. He was very happy to see me there. How was the drive to Milan? And where are you staying?'

'I'm not in Milan,' he answered slowly. 'I'm at our hotel in Venice.'

'In Venice? Why, John? Is the car all right?'

'Yes, it's all right. I'll tell you when I see you. There was a mistake . . .'

He was suddenly so tired, he couldn't tell her about it all. He did not want to talk any more; he couldn't hear Laura very well. He wanted to stop talking, to go to sleep and try to forget about everything.

'Well, what are you going to do? You'll catch the train at Milan tomorrow evening, won't you?'

'Yes, I'll get there,' he told her.

'Well, I must stop now, love,' she said. 'It's dinner time here. Look after yourself and drive carefully.'

30

They said goodbye and he drank some of the wine, stood up and went across to the window. So what's happening? he thought, standing looking out at the little garden at the back of the hotel. I didn't imagine that I saw Laura with those two women in the boat. I know she *was* there, and they were, too. I know it. Are those two women playing games with me? Are they trying to make me believe in them? But why? And what do I do now? Go down and tell the man at the hotel desk that it was all a big mistake? That Laura is in England? He put on his shoes. It was ten to eight.

I'll go to the bar and have a drink, he thought, then I'll talk to the man at the desk, tell him everything is all right. Then perhaps I'll go and tell the police to stop looking for Laura. Say sorry to everyone and leave early in the morning. Get out of the place as quickly as I can.

He went down to the bar and had a quick drink, then he went out to the front desk. It was empty. There was nobody there. He walked on, out into the street. I'll have some dinner somewhere and then tell them later, he told himself. He went to a restaurant near the hotel and sat at a table in the corner and had another half-bottle of wine with his food. It was nearly half-past nine when he finished. He must go and tell them now. He drank his coffee, lit a cigarette and paid.

When he arrived back at the hotel, there was a policeman there. The two sisters were at the police station, he said, and he wanted John to go with him to ask them some questions. John told him and the man at the hotel desk about his mistake, and said he was sorry three or four times, but the policeman was angry and spoke quickly in Italian to the hotel man. John was more and more uncomfortable. He said he was happy to go with the policeman to the police station to see the two sisters and to say sorry to them himself.

31

So he walked back across the Piazza San Marco to the police station, with the angry policeman following him, without a word. The two sisters were there, very unhappy and worried, on chairs in the small office. John told them immediately, and said he was very sorry. The police asked him more difficult questions, angry with him now, not believing his story any more. The two old sisters only wanted to go back to their hotel. They did not want the police to make things difficult for John, and so, after a very uncomfortable half-hour or more, the police let him go. He walked with the two old sisters back to their hotel and tried to tell them about seeing Laura with them in the boat that afternoon.

'Yes, you did see us with her,' the sister with the white hair said, stopping outside their little hotel and looking at him again with her strange, empty eyes, 'but not today. You saw us with her next week. Coming back to Venice, next week. Not today.' She spoke more quietly and slowly than her sister.

'Next week? I don't understand,' said John.

'She sees things that other people cannot see. I told your wife yesterday. But I must take my sister in now. She is very tired. There is nothing for you to say sorry for, you know. My sister and I know that. Goodnight.' And the two old women went into their hotel, leaving him standing outside. The door closed.

He looked round him. Where was he? The square, with another little church in it, was empty and quiet. He looked at the name of the church and thought he knew then where he was. Quite near all the lights and the people of San Marco, he thought – just down that street next to the church . . . He went down the dark little street.

This isn't right, he thought, but then he thought he knew the street. Perhaps I walked down here with Laura yesterday evening, when we were lost. He was nearly at the corner of the street, when he saw the child. It was the same little girl as last night, wearing a dark coat.

Why is she running? he thought. Trying to get away from someone. Afraid.

A man ran into the street behind her, looking round him, looking for her. The little girl ran into a dark door, trying to get away. John stood in another dark door, watching.

The murderer! thought John. He remembered the sudden cry of the night before; a woman dying. This is it again. She's trying to get away from the murderer! He wanted to run away himself, but he could not leave the child to die at the hand of this man. He heard her running again, and suddenly she ran past him, through the dark door where he stood, into the house, not seeing him. What could he do? How could he help her? He ran after her, through the door, now standing open, and into the dark house. He could hear the sound of the murderer, running behind them in the dark. It was too late.

'It's all right,' he called. 'I'll help you.' But she ran on into the house, crying. This is it, he thought. We're in this together now, the child and I. He ran after her, followed her into a room and shut the door behind him, turning the key.

The child was sitting on the floor by the open window of the empty room her coat pulled up over her head.

'It's all right. It's all right now,' he said.

The child stood up fast and pushed the coat back off her head. He looked at her. He could not believe what he saw. Not a child, but a very short, very strong-looking old woman with a big head, not crying now, but smiling at him with dirty teeth. He heard the man outside cry, 'Open the door! Police!'

The woman pulled a long thin knife from her coat and threw it at him as hard as she could . . . No, he thought, I don't want to die like this . . .

and the short woman pulled a long thin knife from her coat and threw it at him as hard as she could. He tried to turn, but it hit him below the ear, on the left.

He saw the boat again, on the Grand Canal, with the two sisters and Laura, looking sad and lost. Not today, not tomorrow, but the day after that. And he knew why they were together, why Laura was back in Venice again. The police started to break down the door, but he could not hear anything now.

No, he thought, I don't want to die like this . . .

ACTIVITIES

Pages 1–5

Before you read

1 Look at the picture on page vi. Where do you think the people are? What are they doing? Look at the man and the woman at the front of the picture. What do you think they are thinking? Look at the two women behind them. What do you think they are talking about?

2 Find these words in your dictionary.

believe empty immediately murderer worried

Now use the words to finish these sentences.

a The mother said to her daughter, 'Go to bed . . . . . .'

b They drank all the wine and threw away the . . . . . bottle.

c The police found the . . . . . and took him to the police station.

d His son was ill in hospital and he was very . . . . . .

e 'I don't . . . . . you! You are wrong!' she shouted angrily.

After you read

3 John and Laura see the two sisters again and again. In which of these places do they see them?

a the restaurant on Torcello

b the church on Torcello

c John and Laura's hotel

d the San Zaccaria church

e the restaurant near San Zaccaria

4 Do you believe that the old sister saw Christine, John and Laura's dead daughter? Do you think that some people can 'see things other people can't see'? Why/why not?

Pages 6–20

Before you read

5 John thinks, 'It's going to be all right.' Do you think John and Laura are going to be happy now? Why/why not?

6 Find these words in your dictionary.

comfortable cry operation

Now find the second half of each sentence on the left from the list on the right.

a They liked the hotel   and ran to find her baby.

b She heard a cry   to have an operation.

c My mother went to hospital   because it was friendly and
                                  comfortable.

After you read

7 Answer these questions:

   a On his evening walk, John hears a strange cry and sees a little
      child. How old is the child? What clothes is she wearing?
      Where does she go?

   b Who is Christine? Laura believes that Christine wants to tell her
      something. What is it?

   c Laura goes back to England. Why? And why does John stay in
      Venice?

8 Work with another student. Have a conversation.

   Student A: You are the old woman with white hair. You are in the
              restaurant. You saw Christine and she spoke to you.
              Tell Laura what she said.

   Student B: You are Laura. Ask the old woman questions about
              Christine and what she said.

Pages 21–35

Before you read

9 Look at the picture on page 23. Where is John? What is he looking
   at? What is he thinking?

10 Find these words in your dictionary.

   imagine   amazed

   a When you think about the future, what do you imagine about
      your life?

   b Are you sometimes amazed by things in the newspaper or on
      television? Tell another student about some of these things.

After you read

11 Who says these words? What is happening?
   a 'No, sir. I'm sorry sir. She is not here.'
   b 'Woman found dead somewhere near here last night.'
   c 'Look after yourself and drive carefully.'
   d 'You saw us with her next week. Not today.'
12 The last words of the story are: 'I don't want to die like this . . .' How do you think John dies? Tell another student.

Writing

13 You are one of the two old sisters. Write a short letter to Laura in England. Tell her what happened to John. Ask her to come to Venice quickly.
14 Write a story about John's murder for the English language newspaper in Venice. Say what happened after the murder.
15 Who do you feel most sorry for in the story: John or Laura. Why?
16 What do you find the most difficult or strangest thing to understand in this story? Why?